Mezzo-Soprano/Belter
Volume 2

MW00914671

THE SINGER'S MUSICAL THEATRE ANTHOLOGY

A collection of songs from the musical stage, categorized by voice type. The selections are presented in their authentic settings, excerpted from the original vocal scores.

Compiled and Edited by Richard Walters

HAL•LEONARD™ CORPORATION
7777 W. BLUEMOUND RD. P.O. BOX 13819 MILWAUKEE, WI 53213

ISBN 0-7935-2330-3

FOREWORD

As the century nears its end, it is apparent to me that the most important and lasting body of performable American music for singers has come from the musical theatre and musical film. The classical tradition as it has been continued in the United States in this century has produced few major composers who have written extensively for the voice, producing a relatively small body of sometimes profound and beautiful literature, but often relevant only to specialized audiences. In pre-rock era popular traditions, the songs that were not written for the stage or film are largely inferior in quality to those written for Broadway and Hollywood (although there are plenty of exceptions to this general rule). Perhaps the reason is simply that the top talent was attracted to and nurtured by those two venues, and inspired by the best performers. But it's also possible that writing for a character playing some sort of scene, no matter how thin the dramatic context (sometimes undetectable), has inherently produced better songs. Compare a Rodgers and Hart ballad from the 1930s (which are all from musicals) to just an average pop ballad from that time not from the stage or screen, if you can dig one up, and you might see what I mean. Popular music of the rock era, primarily performers writing dance music for themselves to record, is almost a completely different aesthetic, and is most often ungratifying for the average singer to present in a typical performance with piano accompaniment.

The five volumes that comprise the original edition of *The Singer's Musical Theatre Anthology,* released in 1987, contain many of the most famous songs for a voice type, as well as being peppered with some more unusual choices. Volume two of the series allows a deeper investigation into the available literature. I have attempted to include a wide range of music, appealing to many different tastes and musical and vocal needs. As in the first volumes, whenever possible the songs are presented in what is their most authentic setting, excerpted from the vocal score or piano/rehearsal score, in the key originally performed and with the original piano accompaniment arrangement (which is really a representation of the orchestra, of course, although Kurt Weill was practically the only Broadway composer to orchestrate his own shows). A student of this subject will notice that these accompaniments are quite a bit different from the standard sheet music arrangements that were published of many of these songs, where the melody is put into a simplified piano part and moved into a convenient and easy piano key, without much regard to vocal range.

In the first volume of the series, I tried to walk a fine line in the mezzo-soprano choices, attempting to accomodate a mix of how theatre people define that voice type —almost exclusively meaning belting — and how classical tradition defines mezzo-soprano. In volume two I have restricted the choices to songs for a belting range, although they don't necessarily need to be belted, and put any songs sung in what theatre people call "head voice" or "soprano voice" in the soprano volume. As was true in the first volume, classically trained mezzo-sopranos will be comfortable with many of the songs in the soprano book.

The "original" keys are presented here, although that often means only the most comfortable key for the original performer. Transpositions of this music are perfectly acceptable. Some songs in these volumes might be successfully sung by any voice type. Classical singers and teachers using these books should remember that the soprano tessitura of this style of material, which often seems very low, was a deliberate aesthetic choice, aimed at clarity of diction, often done to avoid a cultured sound in a singing voice inappropriate to the desired character of the song and role, keeping what I term a Broadway ingenue range. Barbara Cook and Julie Andrews are famous examples of this kind of soprano, with singing concentrated in an expressive and strong middle voice. Also regarding tessituras, some men may find comfortable songs in both the tenor and baritone volumes, in a "baritenor" range, typically with a top note of G.

It's exciting to present songs in this new edition that have never before appeared in print. Many great songs still hold the stage, even if many of the shows don't. The nine volumes of the series present 358 songs from 117 musicals, dating from 1905 to 1991. It's a small percentage of our theatre heritage, but is still a comprehensive and relatively representative sampling of the stage music of New York, and to a much lesser degree London, in the twentieth century.

Many people have been kind and helpful to me in my research and preparation of this edition. They will forgive me if I only mention my debt of gratitude to the late musical theatre historian Stanley Green. I was fortunate enough to work with him as his editor on his last two books. Stanley's grasp of the subject, his compelling prose, and his high standards of research continue to inspire me.

Richard Walters, editor
May, 1993

THE SINGER'S MUSICAL THEATRE ANTHOLOGY
Mezzo-Soprano/Belter
Volume 2

Contents

ABOUT THE SHOWS

ALLEGRO

Music: Richard Rodgers
Lyrics and Book: Oscar Hammerstein II
Director and Choreographer: Agnes de Mille
Opened: 10/10/47, New York; a run of 315 performances

The third Rodgers and Hammerstein Broadway musical, *Allegro* was their first with a story that had not been based on a previous source. It was a particularly ambitious undertaking, with a theme dealing with the corrupting effect of big institutions on the young and idealistic. The saga is told through the life of a doctor, Joseph Taylor Jr., from his birth in a small midwestern town to his 35th year. We follow Joe's progress as he grows up, goes to school, marries a local belle, joins the staff of a large Chicago hospital that panders to wealthy hypochondriacs, discovers that his wife is unfaithful, and, in the end, returns to his home town with his adoring nurse, Emily, to rededicate his life to healing the sick and helping the needy. The show's innovations included a Greek chorus to comment on the action both to the actors and the audience, and the use of multi-level performaing areas with abstract sets. "The Gentleman Is a Dope" is sung by Emily about Joe near the end of the show, just before they declare their affection for one another.

ANYONE CAN WHISTLE

Music and Lyrics: Stephen Sondheim
Book: Arthur Laurents
Director: Arthur Laurents
Choreographer: Herbert Ross
Opened: 4/4/64, New York; a run of 9 performances

Something of a "cult" musical, *Anyone Can Whistle* is an allegorical satire about a corrupt mayor of a bankrupt town who comes up with a scheme to attract tourists: a fake miracle in which a stream of water appears to spout out of a solid rock. The town soon becomes a mecca for the gullible and the pious, but the hoax is exposed when the inmates of a mental institution called the Cookie Jar get mixed up with the pilgrims. Fay is the head nurse at the Cookie Jar, so inhibited that she can't whistle. She sings "There Won't Be Trumpets" about an expectant hero to rescue both her and the situation. The song was cut from the show while on the road and wasn't heard on Broadway. The New York run featured Angela Lansbury in her first Broadway musical, Lee Remick and Harry Guardino.

ANYTHING GOES

Music and Lyrics: Cole Porter
Book: Guy Bolton & P.G. Wodehouse, Howard Lindsay & Russel Crouse
Director: Howard Lindsay
Choreographer: Robert Alton
Opened: 11/21/34, New York; a run of 420 performances

Cole Porter's best score of the 1930s is a fun-filled story taking place on an ocean liner about a group of oddball characters, including a nightclub singer, an enamoured stow away, a debutante, and an underworld criminal disguised as a clergyman. Featuring a fresh, young Ethel Meman, the show was one of the biggest hits of its time, containing such hits as the title song, "You're the Top," "I Get a Kick Out of You," "Blow, Gabriel, Blow," and "All Through the Night." *Anything Goes* played Off Broadway in a 1962 production (239 performances), and enjoyed its biggest success in a 1987 Broadway revival starring Patti LuPone (804 performances). There is a 1936 filmed version, and another movie from 1956 with the title *Anything Goes,* but which bears little resemblance to the original. An excellent new recording, faithful to the 1934 original production, was released in the 1980s featuring Frederica Von Stade, Cris Groenendaal, and Kim Criswell.

The material in this section is by Stanley Green and Richard Walters, some of which was previously published elsewhere.

THE APPLE TREE

Music: Jerry Bock
Lyrics: Sheldon Harnick
Book: Sheldon Harnick, Jerry Bock, Jerome Coopersmith
Director: Mike Nichols
Choreographer: Lee Theodore and Herbert Ross
Opened: 10/18/66, New York; a run of 463 performances

Here was a new concept for Broadway—one musical containing three separate one-act musicals. Though the stories in *The Apple Tree* have nothing in common and, in fact, could be played separately, they are tied together by interrelated musical themes and by the whimsical reference to the color brown. The first act is based on Mark Twain's *The Diary of Adam and Eve,* and dealt with the dawn of humanity and innocence. The second act is based on Frank R. Stockton's celebrated *The Lady or the Tiger?* in which a warrior's fate, unresolved in the story, was determined by the choice of door he enters. The third act is based on Jules Feiffer's *Passionella,* a fantasy about a poor chimney sweep who became a movie star. "Feelings" is sung by Eve in Act I, a bewildering look at first love, literally first love.

BABES IN ARMS

Music: Richard Rodgers
Lyrics: Lorenz Hart
Book: Richard Rodgers and Lorenz Hart
Director: Robert Sinclair
Choreographer: George Balanchine
Opened: 4/14/37, New York; a run of 289 performances

With such songs as "I Wish I Were in Love Again," "Johnny One Note," "The Lady Is a Tramp," "My Funny Valentine," and "Where or When," *Babes in Arms* could claim more hits than any other Rodgers and Hart musical. In the high-spirited, youthful show, a group of teenagers, whose parents are out-of-work vaudevillians, stage a revue to keep from being sent to a work farm. Unfortunately, the show is a bomb. Later, when a transatlantic French flyer lands nearby, they are able to attract enough publicity to put on a successful show and build their own youth center. Because the sets were modest and the cast boasted no stellar names, producer Dwight Deere Wiman priced his tickets at a bargain $3.85 top. In 1959 the plot of the show was revised, the characters names were changed, and the song list slightly altered. (There was never much plot anyway.) The 1939 movie version featured Judy Garland and Mickey Rooney.

BALLROOM

Music: Billy Goldenberg
Lyrics: Alan and Marilyn Bergman
Book: Jerome Kass
Director and Choreographer: Michael Bennett

Ballroom, an extravagant Michael Bennett production, was one of the most expensive productions ever to reach Broadway, highly fanfared before its New York opening, then closed after a very brief run. The spirit of the show rode on the nostalgia wave of the 1970s. "Fifty Percent" was the show's standout song, and has become a standard of sorts in theatre circles.

BELLS ARE RINGING

Music: Jule Styne
Book and Lyrics: Betty Comden and Adolph Green
Director: Jerome Robbins
Choreographers: Jerome Robbins and Bob Fosse
Opened: 11/29/56, New York; a run of 924 performances

Ever since appearing together in a nightclub revue, Betty Comden and Adolph Green had wanted to write a musical for their friend, Judy Holliday. The idea they eventually hit upon was to cast Miss Holliday as a meddlesome operator at a telephone answering service who gets involved with her clients' lives. She is in fact so helpful to one, a playwright in need of inspiration, that they meet, fall in love—though through it all she conceals her true identity—dance and sing in the subway, and entertain fellow New Yorkers in Central Park. At last she confesses that she's the operator, and they go off to loveland. "The Party's Over" is sung when she realizes she has to tell Jeff who she is, and she believes he'll dump her. A film version was made that is virtually the stage show on film, with Dean Martin playing opposite Miss Holliday.

CHESS

Music: Benny Andersson and Bjorn Ulvaeus
Lyrics: Tim Rice
Book: Richard Nelson, based on an idea by Tim Rice
Director: Trevor Nunn
Choreographer: Lynne Taylor-Corbett
Opened: 4/28/88, New York; a run of 68 performances

There have been musicals about the cold war (*Leave it to Me!*, *Silk Stockings*), but *Chess* was the first to treat the conflict seriously, using an international chess match as a metaphor. The idea originated with Tim Rice who first tried to interest his former partner, Andrew Lloyd Webber, in the project. When that failed, he approached Andersson and Ulvaeus, writers and singers with the Swedish pop group ABBA. Like *Jesus Christ Superstar* and *Evita*, *Chess* originated as a successful record album before it became a stage production. Trevor Nunn took over directing the show when Michael Bennett withdrew because of illness. The London production was a high tech spectacle, rock opera type presentation. The libretto was revised for New York, and a different production approach was tried. "Someone Else's Story" was added for the Broadway run. The story is a romantic triangle with a Bobby Fischer type American chess champion, a Russian opponent who defects to the West, and the Hungarian born American woman who transfers her affections from the American to the Russian without bringing happiness to anyone. Though the show ran three years in London, it never made back its initial investment there. It lost $6,000,000 in New York.

A CHORUS LINE

Music: Marvin Hamlisch
Lyrics: Edward Kleban
Book: James Kirkwood and Nicholas Dante
Director and Choreographer: Michael Bennett
Opened: 4/15/75, New York

Beginning with the deceptively simple premise of an audition for chorus dancers, *A Chorus Line* eventually proves to be an interesting examination of the dancer's thoughts and feelings, shown in monologues, dialogues, solo songs, and ensembles. Created as a workshop production in Joseph Papp's Public Theatre, the show, like *Company* and *Follies* before it, has no traditional plot, and has been widely imitated. *A Chorus Line* is the longest running production in Broadway history (exceeded only by the Off Broadway institution, *The Fantasticks*), with a run of 15 years.

COMPANY

Music and Lyrics: Stephen Sondheim
Book: George Furth
Director: Harold Prince
Choreographer: Michael Bennett
Opened: 4/26/70, New York; a run of 706 performances

Company was the first of the Sondheim musicals to have been directed by Harold Prince, and more than any other musical reflects America in the 1970s. The show is a plotless evening about five affluent couples living in a Manhattan apartment building and their excessively protective feeling about a charming, but somewhat indifferent bachelor named Bobby. They want to fix him up and see him married. In the end he seems ready to take the plunge. The songs are often very sophisticated, expressing the ambivalent or caustic attitudes of fashionable New Yorkers.

EVITA

Music: Andrew Lloyd Webber
Lyrics: Tim Rice
Director: Harold Prince
Choreographer: Larry Fuller
Opened: 6/23/78, London; a run of 2,900 performances.
　　　　9/25/79, New York; a run of 1,567 performances

Because of its great success in London, *Evita* was practically a pre-sold hit when it began its run on Broadway. Based on the events in the life of Argentina's strong-willed leader, Eva Peron, the musical—with Patti LuPone in the title role in New York—traced her rise from struggling actress to wife of dictator Juan Peron (Bob Gunton), and virtual co-ruler of the country. Part of the concept of the show is to have a slightly misplaced Che Guevera (played by Mandy Patinkin) as a narrator and conscience to the story of Eva's quick, greedy rise to power and her early death from cancer. "I'd Be Surprisingly Good for You" is what Eva sings to Peron just a minute after their first meeting.

FUNNY GIRL

Music: Jule Styne
Lyrics: Bob Merrill
Book: Isabel Lennart
Directors: Garson Kanin and Jerome Robbins
Choreographer: Carol Haney
Opened: 3/26/64, New York; a run of 1,348 performances

The funny girl of the title refers to Fanny Brice, one of Broadway's legendary clowns, and the story, told mostly in flashback, covers her discovery by impresario Florenz Ziegfeld, her triumphs in the Ziegfeld Follies, her stormy marriage to smooth-talking con man Nick Arnstein, and the breakup of the couple after Nick has served time for stock swindling. Film producer Ray Stark, Miss Brice's son-in-law, had long wanted to make a movie based on the Fanny Brice story, but the original screenplay convinced him that it should first be done on the stage. At one time or another Mary Martin, Carol Burnett, and Anne Bancroft were announced for the leading role, but the assignment went to 22 year old Barbra Streisand, whose only other Broadway experience had been in a supporting part in *I Can Get It For You Wholesale*. However, Streisand, through performances in clubs and on television and recording had already begun her fast ascent to stardom, and she was hardly an unknown on the opening night of *Funny Girl*. The 1968 movie version, directed by William Wyler and Herbert Ross, was Miss Streisand's auspicious film debut.

GOOD NEWS

Music: Ray Henderson
Lyrics: B. G. DeSylva and Lew Brown
Book: Laurence Schwab and B. G. DeSylva
Director: Edgar MacGregor
Choreographer: Bobby Connolly
Opened: 9/6/27, New York; a run of 557 performances

Good News inaugurated a series of bright and breezy DeSylva, Brown and Henderson musical comedies that captured the fast-paced spirit of America's flaming youth of the 1920s. In this collegiate caper, the setting is Tait College where the student body is composed of flappers and sheiks, and where the biggest issue is whether the school's football hero will be allowed to play in the big game against Colton despite his failing grade in astronomy. It's all silly, good natured fun. There was an unsuccessful revival on Broadway in 1974 with Alice Faye and Gene Nelson. The MGM movie version of 1947 starred June Allyson, Peter Lawford and Mel Tormé.

GREASE

Music, Lyrics and Book: Jim Jacobs and Warren Casey
Director: Tom Moore
Choreographer: Patricia Birch
Opened: 2/14/72, New York; a run of 3,388 performances

A surprise runaway hit reflecting the nostalgia fashion of the 1970s, *Grease* is the story of hip greaser Danny and his wholesome girl Sandy Dumbrowski, a loose plot that serves as an excuse for a light-hearted ride through the early rock 'n' roll of the 1950s. The show is currently the third longest running Broadway musical in history, after *A Chorus Line* and *Cats*. The 1978 movie version, starring John Travolta and Olivia Newton-John, is one of the top grossing musical movies of all time.

GUYS AND DOLLS

Music and Lyrics: Frank Loesser
Book: Abe Burrows and Jo Swerling
Director: George S. Kaufman
Choreographer: Michael Kidd
Opened: 11/24/50, New York; a run of 1,200 performances

Populated by the hard-shelled but soft-centered characters who inhabit the world of writer Damon Runyon, this "Musical Fable of Broadway" tells the tale of how Miss Sarah Brown of the Save-a-Soul Mission saves the souls of assorted Times Square riff-raff while losing her heart to the smooth-talking gambler, Sky Masterson. A more comic romance involves Nathan Detroit, who runs the "oldest established permanent floating crap game in New York," and Miss Adelaide, the star of the Hot Box nightclub (where she sings "Take Back Your Mink"), to whom he has been engaged for fourteen years, which explains her famous song, "Adelaide's Lament."

Guys and Dolls played on Broadway for 239 performances with an all black cast in 1976. In 1992, an enormously successful revival opened in New York, and a new cast recording was made of the show, with Faith Prince as Miss Adelaide. The 1955 film version stars Frank Sinatra, Marlon Brando, Jean Simmons, and Vivian Blaine (the original Miss Adelaide).

GYPSY

Music: Jule Styne
Lyrics: Stephen Sondheim
Book: Arthur Laurents
Director and Choreographer: Jerome Robbins
Opened: 5/21/59, New York; a run of 702 performances

Written for Ethel Merman, who gave the performance of her career as Gypsy Rose Lee's ruthless, domineering mother, *Gypsy* is one of the great scores in the mature musical comedy tradition. The idea for the musical began with producer David Merrick, who needed to read only one chapter in Miss Lee's autobiography to convince him of its stage potential. Originally, Stephen Sondheim was to have supplied the music as well as the lyrics, but Miss Merman, who had just come from a lukewarm production on Broadway, wanted the more experienced Jule Styne. In the story, Mama Rose is determined to escape from her humdrum life by pushing the vaudeville career of her daughter June. After June runs away to get married, she focuses all her attention on her other daughter, the previously neglected Louise. After a few years Louise turns into celebrated burlesque stripper Gypsy Rose Lee, and Rose suffers a breakdown when she realizes that she is no longer needed in her daughter's career ("Rose's Turn").

Gypsy also enjoyed a successful London engagement in 1973 with Angela Lansbury as Rose. This production opened in New York the following year and ran for 120 performances. Another revival, celebrating the 30th anniversary of the musical, with Tyne Daley in the Merman role, played in New York beginning in 1989 for 477 performances. (A new cast recording was released). A 1962 film version starred, alas, not Merman but Rosalind Russell.

HOUSE OF FLOWERS

Music: Harold Arlen
Book Lyrics: Truman Capote
Director: Peter Brook
Choreographer: Herbert Ross
Opened: 12/20/54, New York; a run of 165 performances

This "musical Mardi Gras" provided a showcase for the talents of Pearl Bailey as Madame Fleur, a Carribean island madame whose "house of flowers" competed with the house of Madame Tango for the patronage of visiting sailors. Complications result when the girl Violet displays a preference for marrying her sweetheart to being sold to one of Fleur's wealthy clients. Capote wrote a short story based on his visits to the lively bordellos at Port-au-Prince, Haiti, which became the libretto for his only Broadway musical. Ottilie, originally played by Diahann Carroll, is the innocent girl who leaves the temptations of bordello life.

I CAN GET IT FOR YOU WHOLESALE

Music and Lyrics: Harold Rome
Book: Jerome Weidman
Director: Arthur Laurents
Choreographer: Herbert Ross
Opened: 3/22/62, New York; a run of 300 performances

Harry Bogen, the leading character in the show, is an unscrupulous conniver who uses and misuses people on his way to the top. Based on Jerome Weidman's bestselling novel, which the author adapted for the stage, the musical helped two young actors on their way to the top: Elliott Gould, who played Harry, and Barbra Streisand as the comedic, underappreciated secretary, Miss Marmelstein, in a supporting role and her Broadway debut. Set in New York's garment district in the 1930s, Harry rises in the business world through some shady deals until he finally outsmarts himself. At the end, though, there is a hint of redemption when he gets a new job and his estranged sweetheart, Ruthie, comes back to him. In "Who Knows" Ruthie is obviously trying to nudge her relationship with Harry along a bit.

KISS ME, KATE

Music and Lyrics: Cole Porter
Book: Samuel and Bella Spewack
Director: John C. Wilson
Choreographer: Hanya Holm
Opened: 12/30/48, New York; a run of 1,077 performances

The genesis of Cole Porter's longest-running musical occurred in 1935 when producer Saint Subber, then a stagehand for the Theatre Guild's production of Shakespeare's *The Taming of the Shrew,* became aware that its stars Alfred Lunt and Lynn Fontanne, quarreled almost as much in private as did the characters in the play. Years later he offered this parallel story as the basis for a musical comedy to the same writing trio, Porter and the Spewacks, who had already worked on the successful show, *Leave It to Me!* The entire action of *Kiss Me, Kate* occurs backstage and onstage at Ford's Theatre, Baltimore, during a tryout of a musical version of *The Taming of the Shrew.* The main plot concerns the egotistical actor-producer Fred Graham and his temperamental ex-wife Lili Vanessi who —like Shakespeare's Petruchio and Kate— fight and make up and eventually demonstrate their enduring affection for each other. One of the chief features of the score is the skillful way Cole Porter combined his own musical world (songs like "So in Love," "Too Darn Hot," "Why Can't You Behave?") with a Shakespearean world (songs like "I Hate Men"). A screen version from MGM was released in 1953.

MAME

Music and Lyrics: Jerry Herman
Book: Jerome Lawrence and Robert E. Lee
Director: Gene Sachs
Choreographer: Onna White
Opened: 5/24/66, New York; a run of 1,508 performances

Ten years after premiering the comedy based on Patrick Dennis' fictional account of his free-wheeling *Auntie Mame,* play-wrights Lawrence and Lee joined forces with Jerry Herman to transform their play into a hit musical. Angela Lansbury, after years of stage and screen performances, finally achieved her stardom in the title role. The show's big ballad, "If He Walked into My Life," is sung by Mame as she thinks that she's damaged her relationship with her now-grown nephew. A 1983 revival, also starring Miss Lansbury, had a brief run on Broadway. A film version, virtually the last old-fashioned musical movie made, was released in 1974, starring Lucille Ball and Robert Preston, and from the original cast, Bea Arthur. The non-musical film of the story, *Auntie Mame,* was released in 1957 and starred Rosalind Russell.

ME AND JULIET

Music: Richard Rodgers
Lyrics and Book: Oscar Hammerstein II
Director: George Abbott
Choreographer: Robert Alton
Opened: 5/28/53, New York; a run of 358 performances

Me and Juliet was Rodgers and Hammerstein's valentine to show business, with its action — in *Kiss Me, Kate* fashion — taking place both backstage in a theatre and onstage during the performance of a play. Here the tale concerns a romance between a singer in the chorus and the assistant stage manager, whose newfound bliss is seriously threatened by the jealous electrician. A comic romantic subplot invovles the stage manager and the principal dancer. "We Deserve Each Other" is from the play portion of the show, with contemporary Carmen and Don José characters.

MERRILY WE ROLL ALONG

Music and Lyrics: Stephen Sondheim
Book: George Furth
Director: Harold Prince
Choreographer: Larry Fuller
Opened: 11/16/81, New York; a run of 16 performances

Founded on the George S. Kaufman-Moss Hart play of the same name, *Merrily We Roll Along* is an innovative conception in that it tells its tale backwards—from the present when Franklin Shepard is a rich, famous, but morally compromised film producer and composer, to his idealistic youth when he graduated from high school. The story centers around the enduring and changing friendship between 3 people. The Broadway production was not a success, but the tuneful score has gained a following.

LES MISÉRABLES

Music: Claude-Michel Schönberg
Lyrics: Herbert Kretzmer and Alain Boublil
Original French Text: Alain Boublil and Jean-Marc Natel
Directors: Trevor Nunn and John Caird
Choreographer: Kate Flatt
Opened: 9/80, Paris; an initial run of 3 months
          10/8/85 , London; still running as of 6/1/93
          3/12/87, New York; still running as of 6/1/93

Les Misérables lends a pop opera texture to the 1200 page Victor Hugo epic novel of social injustice and the plight of the downtrodden. The original Parisian version contained only a few songs, and many more were added when the show opened in London. Thus, most of the show's songs were originally written in English. The plot is too rich to capsulize, but centers on Jean Valjean, who has go to prison in previous years for stealing a loaf of bread, and takes place over several years in the first half of the 19th century. "I Dreamed a Dream" is sung by Fantine, ill and dying. Cosette, secretly in love with Marius, sings "Own My Own."

THE MYSTERY OF EDWIN DROOD

Music, Lyrics and Book: Rupert Holmes
Director: Wilford Leach
Choreographer: Graciela Daniele
Opened: 12/2/85, New York; a run of 608 performances

Rupert Holmes' lifelong fascination with Charles Dickens' unfinished novel was the catalyst for the play. Since there were no clues as to Drood's murderer or even if a murder had been committed, Holmes decided to let the audience provide the show's ending by voting how it turns out. The writer's second major decision was to offer the musical as if it were being performed by an acting company at London's Music Hall Royale in 1873, complete with such conventions as a Chairman (George Rose) to comment on the action and a woman (Betty Buckley) to play the part of Edwin Drood. The show was notable for the appearance of jazz legend Cleo Laine as the eccentric and mysterious Princess Puffer. On November 13, 1986, in an attempt to attract more theatre-goers, the musical's title was changed to *Drood.*

NINE

Music & Lyrics: Maury Yeston
Book: Arthur Kopit, Mario Fratti
Director: Tommy Tune
Choreographers: Tommy Tune & Thommie Walsh
Opened: 5/9/82, New York; a run of 732 performances

The influence of the director-choreographer was emphasized again with Tommy Tune's highly stylized, visually striking production of *Nine,* which, besides being a feast for the eyes is also one of the very few non-Sondheim Broadway scores to have true musical substance and merit from the 1970s and 1980s. The musical evolved from Yeston's fascination with Federico Fellini's semi-autobiographical 1963 film *8 1/2.* The story spotlights Guido Contini, a celebrated but tormented director in a mid-life crisis who has come to a Venetian spa for a rest, and his relationships with his wife, his mistress, his protégé, his producer, and his mother. Luisa, Guido's wife, sings about her unusual husband near the beginning of the show in "My Husband Makes Movies."

NO STRINGS

Music and Lyrics: Richard Rodgers
Book: Samuel Taylor
Director & Choreographer: Joe Layton
Opened: 3/15/62, New York; a run of 580 performances

Richard Rodgers' first musical after the death of his partner, Oscar Hammerstein II, and the only Broadway production in his long career for which the composer also served as his own lyricist. *No Strings* offered such innovations as hiding the orchestra backstage, featuring instrumentalists onstage to accompany the singers, having the principals and chorus move scenery and props in full view of the audience, and—to conform to the play's title—eliminating the orchestra's string section. The libretto is of a love affair between a fashion model (Diahann Carroll), and a former Pulitzer Prize-winning novelist, now a "Europe bum" (Richard Kiley). In the end, after enjoying the good life in Monte Carlo, Honfleir, Deauville, and St. Tropez, the writer, with no strings attached, reutrns home to the U.S. Though because of casting, the show was about an interracial romance, this was never commented on in the script. "The Sweetest Sounds" opens the show, sung as a kind of an overture to the evening.

OLIVER!

Music, Lyrics and Book: Lionel Bart
Director: Peter Coe
Opened: 6/30/60, London; a run of 2,618 performances
　　　　　1/6/63, New York; a run of 744 performances

Oliver! established Lionel Bart as Britain's outstanding musical theatre talent of the 1960s when the musical opened in London. Until overtaken by *Jesus Christ Superstar, Oliver!* set the record as the longest running musical in British history. Based on Charles Dickens' novel about the orphan Oliver Twist and his adventures as one of Fagin's pickpocketing crew, *Oliver!* also had the longest run of any British musical presented in New York in the 1960s. The show was revived on Broadway in 1984. In 1968, it was made into an Academy Award winning movie produced by Columbia. "As Long As He Needs Me" is Nancy's song about her rough and abusive man, Bill Sykes.

ONCE UPON A MATTRESS

Music: Mary Rodgers
Lyrics: Marshall Barer
Book: Jay Thompson, Dean Fuller and Marshall Barer
Director: George Abbott
Choreographer: Joe Layton
Opened: 5/11/59, New York; a run of 460 performances

Once Upon a Mattress was first created as a one act musical by Mary Rodgers (daughter of Richard Rodgers) and Marshall Barer at an adult summer camp. They expanded the work, based on the fairy tale "The Princess and the Pea," into a full evening's entertainment that is notable as the stage debut of Carol Burnett as Princess Winnifred. Queen Agravain has ruled that her son will only marry someone of royal blood. Winnifred spends a sleepless night, disturbed by one lone pea, planted by the queen, under a pile of mattresses. Actually, an accomplice had secretly stuffed the bed with an arsenol of uncomfortability. In "Shy" Princess Winnifred introduces herself.

PETER PAN

Music: Mark Charlap, additional music by Jule Styne
Lyrics: Carolyn Leigh, additional lyrics by Betty Comden and Adolph GreenDirector and Choreographer: Jerome Robbins
Opened: 10/20/54, New York; a run of 152 performances

Although many actresses have portrayed Peter Pan in almost as many productions, Mary Martin and this version of the story are perhaps the best known and loved. In spite of a modest run on Broadway, this production found a vast new audience through numerous television broadcasts. Peter Pan was first presented in New York in 1905 with Maude Adams as Peter, revived in 1924 with Marilyn Miller, who added two Jerome Kern songs to the show. In 1950 Jean Arthur played Peter to Boris Karloff's Captain Hook, with five songs by Leonard Bernstein. A 1979 revival of the 1954 musical ran 551 performances and starred Sandy Duncan.

PLAIN AND FANCY

Music: Albert Hague
Lyrics: Arnold B. Horwitt
Book: Joseph Stein and Will Glickman
Director: Morton Da Costa
Choreographer: Helen Tamiris
Opened: 1/27/55, New York; a run of 461 performances

The setting of *Plain and Fancy* was Amish country in Pennsylvania, where two worldly New Yorkers (Richard Derr and Shirl Conway) have gone to sell a farm they ahd inherited—but not before they had a chance to meet the God-fearing people and appreciate their simple but unyielding way of living. The warm and atmospheric score was composed by Albert Hague, familiar to television viewers as the bearded music teacher in the series *Fame*.

THE SECRET GARDEN

Music: Lucy Simon
Lyrics & Book: Marsha Norman
Director: Susan H. Schulman
Choreographer: Michael Lichtefeld
Opened: 4/25/91, New York; a run of 706 performances

Based on the novel by Frances Hodgson Burnett, the story is of an orphaned child, Mary Lennox, who is sent to live with her uncle Archibald in Yorkshire in the nineteenth century. He is absorbed in grief over the death of his young wife ten years earlier, and the house is gloomy and mysterious. Mary finds her dead aunt's "secret garden," passionately nurtures it to life, and Archie also comes back to life once he can let go of his grief. The song "Hold On" is sung by the warm and caring servant Martha, in her local Yorkshire accent, to the frightened and insecure Mary.

SHE LOVES ME

Music: Jerry Bock
Lyrics: Sheldon Harnick
Book: Joe Masteroff
Director: Harold Prince
Choreographer: Carol Haney
Opened: 4/23/63, New York; a run of 301 performances

The closely integrated, melody drenched score of *She Loves Me* is certainly one of the best ever written for a musical comedy. It was based on a Hungarian play, *Parfumerie,* by Miklos Laszlo, that had already been used as the basis for two films, *The Shop Around the Corner* and *In the Good Old Summertime* (with a change of locale to the U.S.) Set in the 1930s in what could only be Budapest, the tale is of the people who work in Maraczek's Parfumerie, principally the constantly quabbling sales clerk Amalia Balash (Barbara Cook) and the manager Georg Nowack (Daniel Massey). It is soon revealed that they are anonymous pen pals who agree to meet one night at the Café Imperiale, though neither knows the other's identity. Ilona is an illiterate clerk at the store, a comic but attractive recipient of the attention of men. Taking the advice of her friend, Amalia, she makes a trip to the library, and well...The musical is well represented on the original cast album, which on two disks preserves practically every note of the show's music.

SONG AND DANCE

Music: Andrew Lloyd Webber
Lyrics: Don Black, Richard Maltby Jr.
Adaptation: Richard Maltby Jr.
Director: Richard Maltby Jr.
Choreographer: Peter Martins
Opened: 9/18/85, New York; a run of 474 performances

The "Dance" of the title originated in 1979 when Andrew Lloyd Webber composed a set of variations on Paganini's A minor Capriccio that seemed to him to be perfect for a ballet. The "Song" originated a year later with a one-woman television show, *Tell Me on a Sunday,* which consisted entirely of musical pieces. Two years after that both works were presented together in London as a full evening's entertainment, now connected with a bit of plot. In New York, this unconventional package won high praise for Bernadette Peters, whose task in Act I was to create, without dialogue or other actors, the character of a free-spirited English girl who has dalliances in America with four men.

SUNDAY IN THE PARK WITH GEORGE

Music and Lyrics: Stephen Sondheim
Book and Direction: James Lapine
Opened: 5/2/84, New York; a run of 604 performances

The centerpiece of this ambitious show is George Seurat's great painting "A Sunday Afternoon on the Island of La Grande Jatte." It is an intimate and personal musical concerned with the creative process itself, its obsessions, consequences, and rewards. The piece received the Pulitzer Prize for drama in 1985. An adaptation of the Broadway production (starring Mandy Patinkin and Bernadette Peters) was made for television, and is available for purchase on videotape. "Everybody Loves Louis," sung by Dot after she and George have split up, is about her new beau, Louis, the baker.

THEY'RE PLAYING OUR SONG

Music: Marvin Hamlisch
Lyrics: Carole Bayer Sager
Book: Neil Simon
Director: Robert Moore
Choreographer: Patricia Birch
Opened: 2/11/79, New York; a run of 1,082 performances

They're Playing Our Song was based in part on composer Marvin Hamlisch's often tempestuous romance with lyricist Carole Bayer Sager. In the quasi-drame à clef musical, Vernon Gersch, a wise-cracking neurotic song writer, and Sonia Walsk, a wise-cracking, neurotic lyric writer, try to have both a professional and personal relationship, despite constant interruptions caused by telephone calls from Sonia's former lover. To tell their story, the authors hit upon the notion of having only two real characters in the musical, though each has three singing alter egos, and their songs express how they feel about their work as well as about each other.

THERE WON'T BE TRUMPETS

from *Anyone Can Whistle*

Words and Music by
STEPHEN SONDHEIM

He may ___ not be the cav - a - lier, Tall and ___

54

___ grace - ful, Fair and ___ strong. Does - n't mat - ter ___

___ just as long as he comes a - long! _____ But

Marcia *(accel. poco ma non troppo)*

not with trum - pets or light - ning flash - es Or

won't be trum-pets, but sure as shoot-ing, You'll

know him when you see him!

Faster (♩.=88)

Don't know when, Don't know where, And I

(sempre cresc.)

can't e-ven say that I care! All I know is, the

I GET A KICK OUT OF YOU
from *Anything Goes*

Words and Music by
COLE PORTER

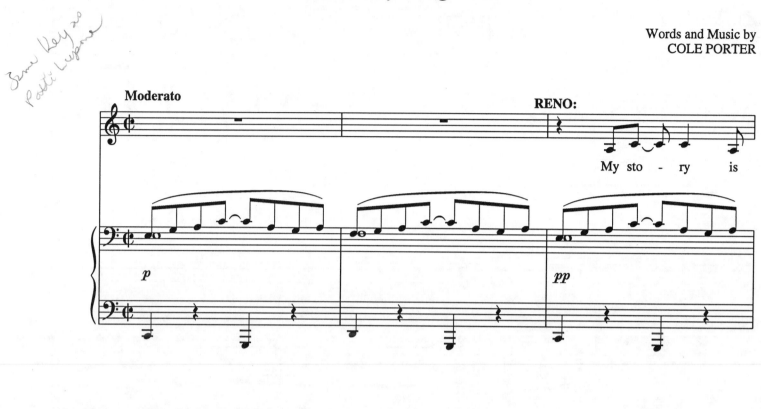

26

guy in the sky Is my i - dea of noth - ing to do, Yet I get a kick out of you.

FEELINGS
from *The Apple Tree*

Words and Music by JERRY BOCK
and SHELDON HARNICK

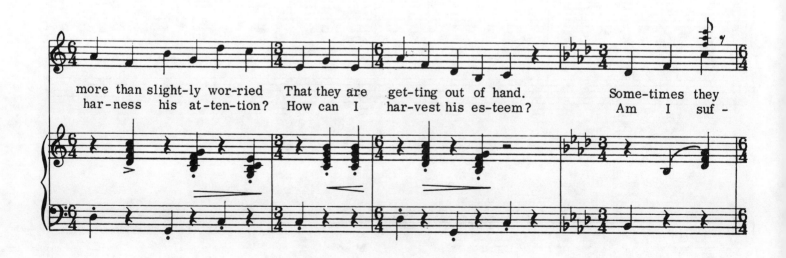

THE GENTLEMAN IS A DOPE

from *Allegro*

Lyrics by OSCAR HAMMERSTEIN II
Music by RICHARD RODGERS

meno mosso

He is-n't ver-y smart___ He's just a lug, you'd

like to hug and hold a-gainst your heart. The gen-tle-man does-n't know___

_R.H._ How hap-py he could be ___ Look at me! Cry-ing my

_L.H._

eyes out, As if he be-longed to me! ___ He'll

I WISH I WERE IN LOVE AGAIN

from *Babes in Arms*

Lyrics by LORENZ HART
Music by RICHARD RODGERS

Moderato

TERRY:

The sleep-less nights, The dai-ly fights, The quick to-bog-gan when you reach the heights, I miss the kiss-es and I miss the bites. I wish I were in love a-gain! The bro-ken dates, The end-less waits, The

This is a duet in the show.

(Tempo primo)

The fur - tive sigh, The black-ened eye, The words "I'll love you till the

day I die," The self de - cep - tion that be - lieves the lie, I wish I were in

love a - gain! When love con - geals it soon re - veals the faint a - ro - ma of per-

form - ing seals, The dou - ble cross-ing of a pair of heels, I wish I were in

love a-gain! No _ more care, No _ des - pair,

I'm _ all there now, _ But I'd rath - er be punch drunk! _ Be -

lieve me, sir, I much pre - fer the clas - sic bat - tle of a him and her, I

don't like qui - et and I wish I were in love a - gain!

JOHNNY ONE NOTE
from *Babes in Arms*

Words by LORENZ HART
Music by RICHARD RODGERS

48

FIFTY PERCENT
from *Ballroom*

Lyrics by ALAN and MARILYN BERGMAN
Music by BILLY GOLDENBERG

THE PARTY'S OVER

from *Bells Are Ringing*

Words by BETTY COMDEN and ADOLPH GREEN
Music by JULE STYNE

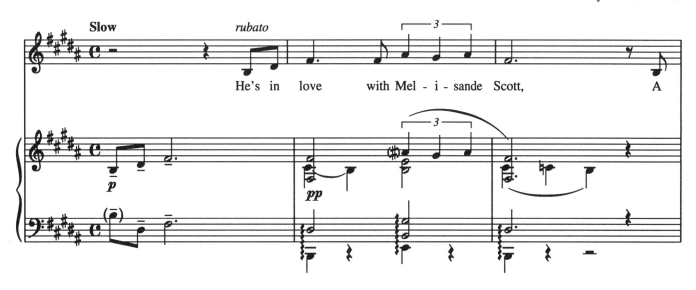

He's in love with Mel - i - sande Scott, A

girl who does-n't ex - ist. He's in love with some-one you're not, and

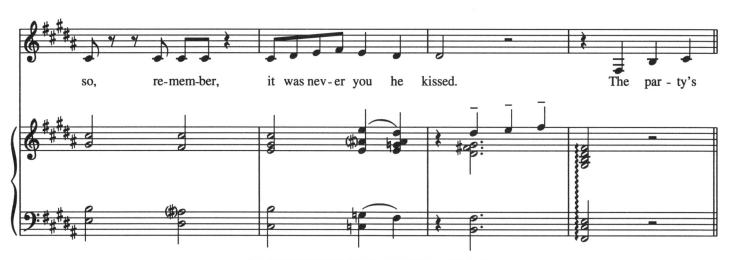

so, re-mem-ber, it was nev-er you he kissed. The par-ty's

o - ver. It's time to call it a day. _____ No mat - ter

how you pre-tend, you knew it would end this way. It's time to wind up

the mas-quer - ade. Just make your mind up the pi - per

must be paid. The par - ty's o - ver, The can - dles flick - er and dim. _____

poco rit.　　a tempo　　p

LONG BEFORE I KNEW YOU
from *Bells Are Ringing*

Lyrics by BETTY COMDEN
and ADOLPH GREEN
Music by JULE STYNE

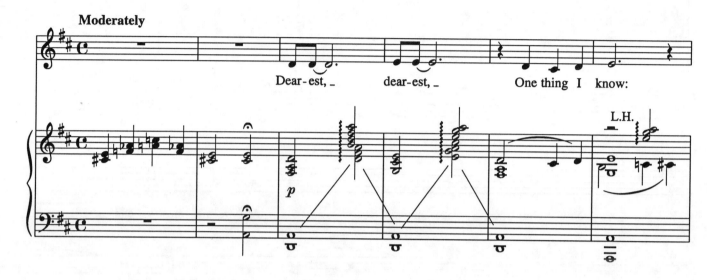

*In the show Ella sings portions of this song, but never the entire number.

I was sure I'd find you ____ Some day, some - how. ____

I pic - tured some - one who'd walk and talk and smile as you do, Who'd

make me feel as you do right now. ____ All that was

long be - fore I held you, ____ Long be - fore I kissed you, ____

Long be-fore I touched you_____ and felt this glow._____

But now you real-ly are here and

now at last I know That long be-fore I knew you,___

___ I loved you so.

SOMEONE ELSE'S STORY
from *Chess*

Words and Music by
BENNY ANDERSSON, TIM RICE
and BJORN ULVAEUS

Slow 8 - Beat Ballad

FLORENCE:

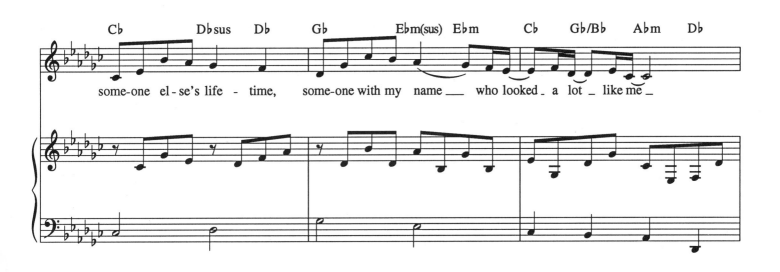

WHAT I DID FOR LOVE

from *A Chorus Line*

Lyrics by EDWARD KLEBAN
Music by MARVIN HAMLISCH

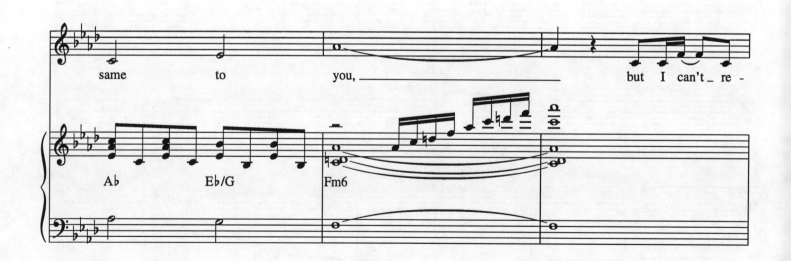

ANOTHER HUNDRED PEOPLE

from *Company*

Music and Lyrics by
STEPHEN SONDHEIM

off of the train __ and the plane and the bus __ may - be yes-ter - day. _____

It's a ci - ty of strang - ers. _____

Some come to work, some __ to play. __ A ci - ty of strang - ers, _____

Some come to stare, some __ to stay. _____ And

ev - 'ry day _____ the ones who stay _____

(poco cresc.)

can find each oth - er in the crowd - ed streets and the

mp

guard - ed parks, _____ By the rust - y foun - tains and the

dust - y trees with the bat - tered barks, _____ And they

looked in vain? Can we see each oth-er Tues-day if it does-n't rain?__ Look, I'll

call you in the morn-ing or my ser-vice will ex-plain.__

poco cresc.

(dim.)

And an-

oth-er hun-dred peo-ple just got off of the train.__

p

dim. poco a poco

molto rit.

ppp

THE MUSIC THAT MAKES ME DANCE

from *Funny Girl*

Words by BOB MERRILL
Music by JULE STYNE

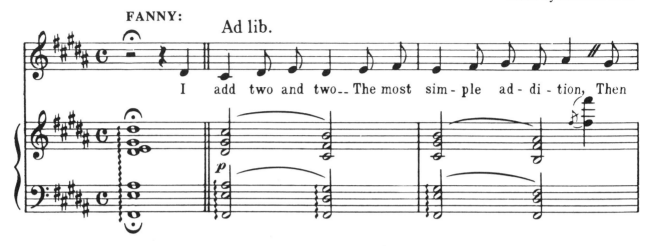

vance. His words and his words a - lone are the words that can start my heart sing - ing. ___ And his is the on - ly mu - sic that makes me dance. ___ He'll sleep and he'll rise in the light of two eyes that a -

dore him.   Bore him it might, But he

won't leave my sight for a glance.   In ev-'ry

way, ev-'ry day, I need less of my-self And need more him.

Ad lib.

more him._____ 'Cause his is the on - ly mu - sic that makes me

colla voce

dance._____ 'Cause his is the on - ly

Br.

mu - sic that makes me dance!_____

I'D BE SURPRISINGLY GOOD FOR YOU

from *Evita*

Lyrics by TIM RICE
Music by ANDREW LLOYD WEBBER

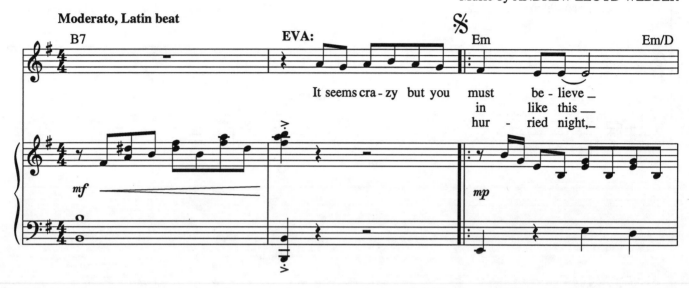

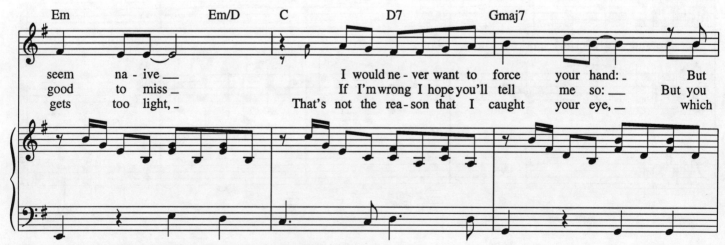

The accompaniment has been written out as a simple suggestion of the style.
It's most appropriate for the pianist to improvise in a gentle Latin style.

MCA music publishing

I WANT TO BE BAD
from *Good News*

Lyrics and Music by
B.G. DeSYLVA, LEW BROWN
and RAY HENDERSON

Good or bad which is the best for me?

marc.

When you're af - ter fun and laugh - ter This ag - gra - vates___ you

8vb

Some re-form - er says a warm - er cli-mate a - waits___ you.

8vb

Refrain

If it's naught-y to rouge your lips___ Shake your should-ers and twist your hips___

p - f rhythmic

LOOK AT ME, I'M SANDRA DEE

from *Grease*

Lyric and Music by WARREN CASEY
and JIM JACOBS

* Sung an octave lower than written

89

90

nev - er stoop so low, please keep your cool, now you're
start - ing to drool, fon - gool, I'm San - dra Dee.

ADELAIDE'S LAMENT
from *Guys and Dolls*

By FRANK LOESSER

grippe, (Hm!) La grippe, La post na-sal drip With the whee-zes and the sneezes and a

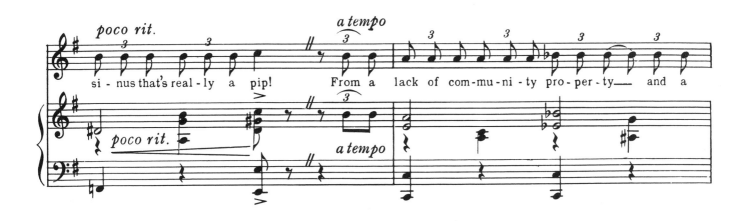

si-nus that's real-ly a pip! From a lack of com-mu-ni-ty pro-per-ty___ and a

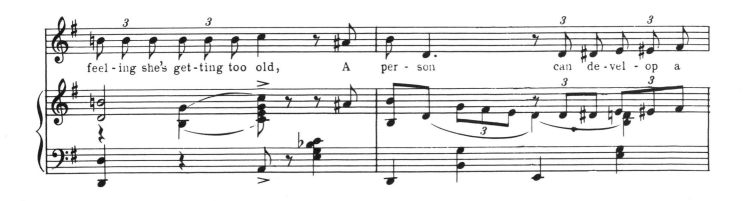

feel-ing she's get-ting too old, A per-son can de-vel-op a

bad bad cold. ___

SMALL WORLD

from *Gypsy*

Words by STEPHEN SONDHEIM
Music by JULE STYNE

I HATE MEN

from *Kiss Me, Kate*

Words and Music by
COLE PORTER

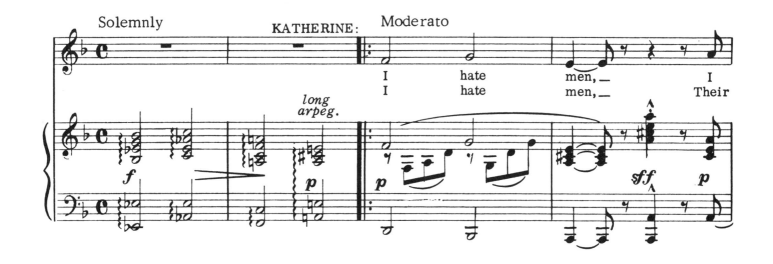

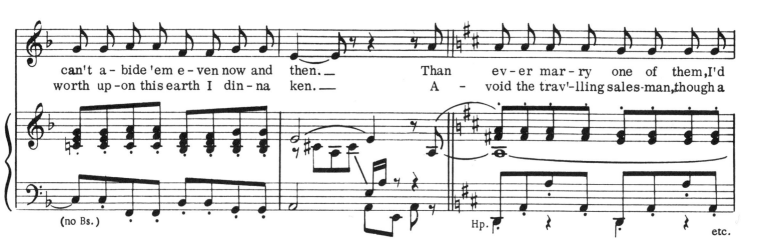

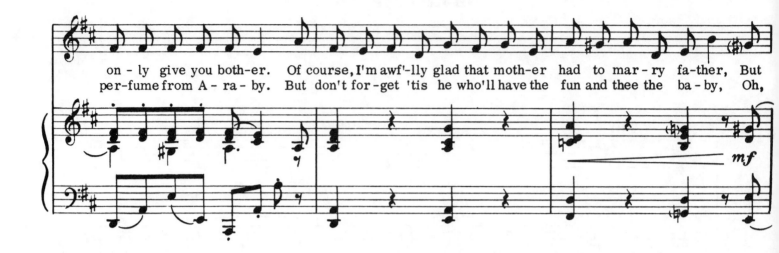

on - ly give you both-er. Of course, I'm awf'-lly glad that moth-er had to mar - ry fa-ther, But
per-fume from A - ra - by. But don't for-get 'tis he who'll have the fun and thee the ba - by, Oh,

Cantabile

Gaily

I ____ hate men. ___ Of all the types I've ev - er met, with-
I ____ hate men. ___ If thou shouldst wed a bus'-ness man, Be

in our de - mo - cra - cy, I hate the most, the ath - lete with his
wa - ry, oh be wa - ry, He'll tell you he's de - tained in town on

man - ner bold and brass - y. He may have hair up - on his chest, But
bus' - ness nec - es - sar - y. His bus' - ness is the bus' - ness which he

sis - ter, so has Las - sie, Oh, I ____ hate men! __
gives his sec - re - ta - ry, Oh, I ____ hate men! __

men! __
men! __

I NEVER HAS SEEN SNOW
from *House of Flowers*

Lyrics by TRUMAN CAPOTE
and HAROLD ARLEN
Music by HAROLD ARLEN

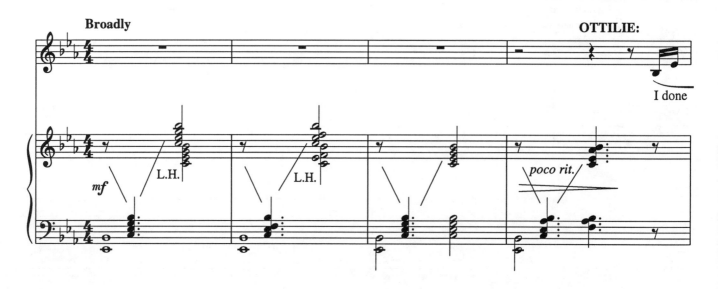

closed the door on the girl I was be - fore.

p

Feel-in' fine and full o' bliss, what I real - ly wants to say is this:

p *rit.* *a tempo*

8va

ff

I

nev - er has seen snow, all the same I know,

p

Snow ain't so beau-ti-ful,_____ C'ain't be so beau-ti-ful like my

love is,_____ Like my love is.

Noth - in' do com-pare Noth - in' an - y-where with

my love._____ A hun - dred things I see,_____

A stone rolled off my heart when I laid my eyes on

that near to me boy with that far a - way look, __ and right from the start, __ I

saw a new hor - i - zon and a road to take me where I want - ed to be took, __

need - ed to be took, __ and

WHO KNOWS
from *I Can Get It For You Wholesale*

Words and Music by
HAROLD ROME

Freely

RUTHIE:

New York is a won-der-ful town, A ver-y stim-u-lat-ing place to be. It's full of gal-ler-ies and ex-hi-bi-tions, Most are ab-so-lute-ly free, And con-certs like at Lew-is-ohn sta-di-um, plus at Car-ne-gie hall. We sit 'way up top, but it's won-der-ful a-cous-tics. That's where it sounds best of

all. Art lec-tures at the Met-ro- pol-i-tan. I at-

tend-ed an-cient Greece the oth-er day. The mod-ern dance and

Fls.

bal-let at the Y. M. and Dou-ble-u H. A. And le - git-i-mate plays on

Broad-way. Don't you think O-dets is great? Not down stairs, of course, We get

last min-ute bal-co-ny down at Gray's Cut Rate. What bet-ter way can a

single girl, with lei-sure spare time find, Than to go a-round, broad-en

out her back-ground, Al-so im-prove her mind? Plus it gives more chance for

meet-ing up with peo-ple, would-n't you say? Such as cer-tain mem-bers of the

op-po-site sex she hopes to get in-volved with some day. And who can

In 2

tell?_____ Who knows _____ when they might

Fls.

Str.

Bsn.

Cello

Tempo - In 4

come _____ one's way?_____ Who

Celeste, Fls.

knows _____ when I'll see him, who knows?_____ Or

W.W.

L.H. *L.H.*

Str.

mp

day he'll see me there and hold out his arms.

Tempo rubato

First he'll kiss me, Say he loves me. And then pro-pose! But

why, where, when, Who knows?

IF HE WALKED INTO MY LIFE

from *Mame*

Music and Lyric by
JERRY HERMAN

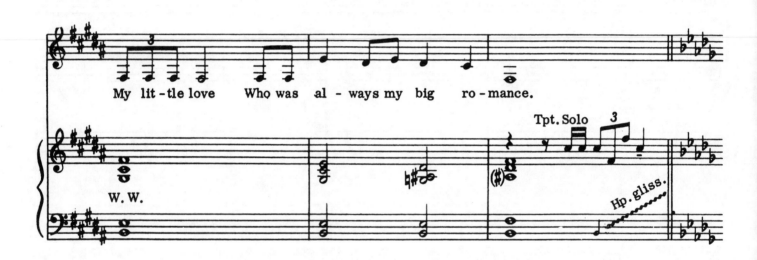

child? And there must have been a mil - lion things

That my heart for-got to say. Would I think of one or

two___ if he walked in - to my life ___ to - day? ___

___ Should I blame the times I pam - pered him or blame the times I

bossed him? ____ What a shame I nev-er real - ly found the

poco accel.

boy be - fore I lost him. Were the years a lit - tle

rall. Tpts. Trbs. 3 33 +Hp.gliss. p W.W.,Tbn's.

fast? — Str'gs,E.H.,(or Cl.) Was his world a lit -tle free? ____

Hp.,Guit.

Was there too much of a crowd, All too lush and loud And not e-nough of

me? Tho' I'll ask my-self my whole life long,

What went wrong a-long the way? Would I make the same mis-

takes___ If he walked in-to my life _____ to - day? _____ If that

boy___ with the bu-gle   Walked in - to   my   life,   to -

Faster

day? _____

WE DESERVE EACH OTHER
from *Me and Juliet*

Lyrics by OSCAR HAMMERSTEIN II
Music by RICHARD RODGERS

Moderato

We de-serve each oth-er, We de-serve each oth-er,

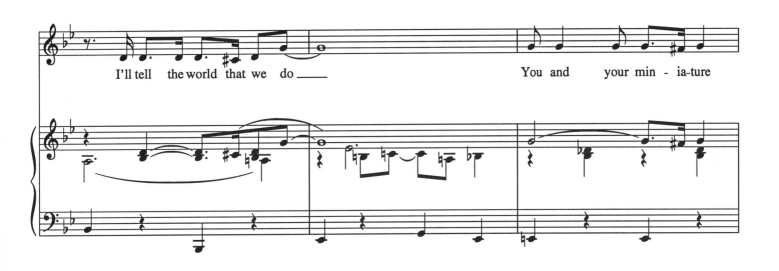

I'll tell the world that we do ___ You and your min-ia-ture

spar-row brain, ___ I and my ti-ny I. Q. We de-serve each oth-er,

Let me tell you, broth-er, I am a dif - fi-cult girl. ___

You're an im - pos - si - ble char - ac - ter, ___ Why don't we give it a

whirl? I don't want _ to re - form you, ___ To

make your mis - takes _ you are free. But I just want _ to be

cer - tain ___ that your great-est mis-take will be me!

If you want to wres-tle, I'm the weak-er ves-sel, And I'll be eas - y to swerve, ___

___ We de - serve each oth - er, ___ So

let us take what we de - serve.

NOW YOU KNOW

from *Merrily We Roll Along*

Music and Lyrics by
STEPHEN SONDHEIM

MARY:

All right, now you know:

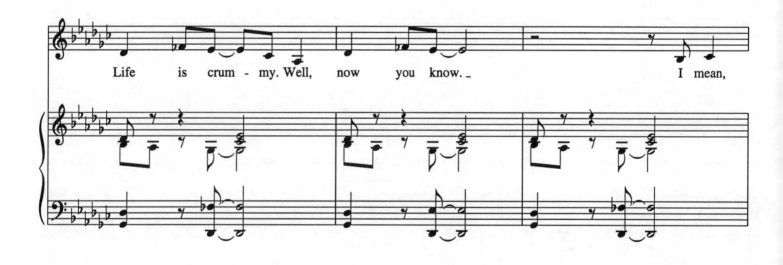

Life is crum-my. Well, now you know._ I mean,

big sur-prise: Peo-ple love_ you and tell you lies.

now and then __ Or you'll nev - er grow! _____ Be-cause

now you grow. __ That's the kill - er is, Now you grow. __

You're right, noth - ing's fair, __ And it's all a plot, __ And to -

mor - row does - n't look too hot — Right, you bet - ter look at

(Pause, as he doesn't respond.)

what you've got: _____

O - ver

(Frank looks at her, smiles for the first time.)

here, hel - lo? _____

O - kay, now you know. _____

_____

Right?

I DREAMED A DREAM
from *Les Misérables*

Lyrics by HERBERT KRETZMER
Original Text by ALAIN BOUBLIL and JEAN-MARC NATEL
Music by CLAUDE-MICHEL SCHÖNBERG

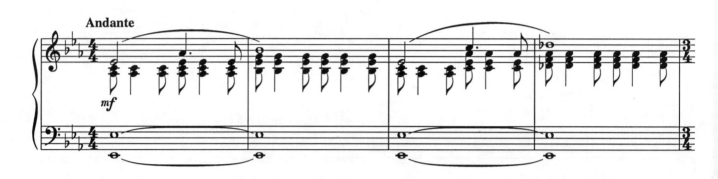

And the song was ex -cit -ing. There was a time. Then it all went wrong.

Andante

FANTINE:

I dreamed a dream in time gone by When hope was high and life worth

liv - ing, I dreamed that love would nev - er die,

I dreamed that God would be for - giv-ing.

Then I was young and un - af -

raid

And dreams were made and used and wast-ed.

There was no ran - som to be paid,

No song un-sung, no wine un -

Poco più mosso

tast - ed.

But the ti - gers come at night

mf

With their voi - ces soft as thun - der,

As they tear your hope a -

part,

As they turn your dream to shame.

rall.   *a tempo*

He slept a sum - mer by my

side,

He filled my days with end - less won - der,

He took my child-hood in his stride

But he was gone when au-tumn

poco accel.

Più mosso

came.

cresc.

And still I dreamed he'd come to

mf

(8vb ad lib.)

me.

That we would live the years to - geth - er.

But there are dreams that can - not be

And there are storms we can-not

weath-er.

I had a dream my life would

cresc.

f appassionato

be

So dif-f'rent from this hell I'm liv - ing,_ So dif-f'rent now from what it

cresc.

poco rall.

a tempo

seemed.

Now life has killed the dream I dreamed.

ff   dim.

p

rall.

ON MY OWN
from *Les Misérables*

Lyrics by HERBERT KRETZMER, JOHN CAIRD and TREVOR NUNN
Original Text by ALAIN BOUBLIL and JEAN-MARC NATEL
Music by CLAUDE-MICHEL SCHÖNBERG

EPONINE:

And now I'm all a-lone a-gain, no-where to go, no one to turn to.

I did not want your mon-ey sir, I came out here 'cos I was told to, And now the night is

near, Now I can make be - lieve he's here.

Some-times I walk a-lone at night when ev-ery-bod-y else is sleep - ing,

I think of him and then I'm hap-py with the com-pa-ny I'm keep - ing. The ci - ty goes to

rall.   Andante

bed   And I can live in - side my head.

On my own,   pre - tend - ing he's be -
rain,   the pave - ment shines like

side _ me,   All a - lone   I walk with him 'til
sil - ver,   All the lights   are mis - ty in the

morn - ing.   With - out him   I feel his arms a -
riv - er.   In the dark - ness,   the trees are full of

love him, _____ but when the night is o - ver _____ he is gone, the riv - er's just a riv - er. With - out him the world a - round me chang - es. The trees are bare and ev - 'ry - where the streets are full of strang - ers. I

love him, ___ but ev-'ry day I'm learn-ing, ___ all my life I've on-ly been pre-

tend-ing. ___ With-out me his world will go on turn-ing, The

world is full of hap-pi-ness that I have nev-er known. I love him, ___ I

love him, ___ I love him, ___ but on-ly on my own.

THE WAGES OF SIN
from *The Mystery of Edwin Drood*

Words and Music by
RUPERT HOLMES

thrup-pence, or you slut to cop some sleep, bash a face for bleed-in'

tup-pence... pure dis-grace to work so cheap. So I say, don't be a

sin-ner for the price of Lon-don gin. You can't pay for one square

din-ner with the wa-ges of sin; sell my soul? 'Cor love, come

Rubato

off it! Who would buy this sack of skin? On the whole there ain't much

pro - fit in the wa - ges of sin, in the wa - ges of

sin, in _____ the wa - ges of sin! I've seen

Tempo I

girls from gut - ter fam' - lies trap rich men wiv flut - t'ry ways, and they

coo, "Cor, pass the jam, please" ov - er nup - tial break-fast trays. Ov - er

there, in bed e - lev - en sleeps a bleed - in' hy - po - crite, spends his

days eyes cast to 'ea - ven: spends his nights a-mongst this shit — S'why I

say, don't take half - meas-ures. Do things right and dig right in. In this

MY HUSBAND MAKES MOVIES

from *Nine*

Lyrics and Music by
MAURY YESTON

Tempo II (♩ = 68)

Gui - do Con - ti - ni, Lu - i - sa Con - ti - ni; num - ber one gen - ius and num - ber one fan.

Gui - do Con - ti - ni, Lu - i - sa Con - ti - ni; daugh-ter of well - to-do Flor - en - tine clan long a -

rit.

go twen-ty years a - go. Once the names were

a tempo

Gui - do Con - ti - ni, Lu - i - sa Del For - no; ac - tress with dreams and a life of her own,

Pas-sion-ate, wild, and in love in Li-vor-no, sing-ing with Gui-do all night on the phone long a-

go some-one else a-go. How he needs me

so, and he'll be the last to know it. My

Tempo I

hus - band makes mov - ies. To

make them, he makes him-self ob-sessed. He works for

weeks on end with-out a bit of rest no oth - er

way can he a-chieve his lev-el best.

Some men read books, some shine their shoes,

some re-tire __ ear-ly when they've seen the eve-ning news. My

hus-band on-ly rare-ly comes to bed my

rit.

hus-band makes mov-ies, in-stead. My

Tempo II

hus-band makes mov-ies...

8va bassa

THE SWEETEST SOUNDS
from *No Strings*

Lyrics and Music by
RICHARD RODGERS

BARBARA:

What do I real-ly hear _____ And what is in the ear of my mind? Which sounds are true and clear _____ And which will nev-er be de-fined? The

The verse does not appear in the show, but was written by Mr. Rodgers for the song to stand alone.

dear - est love in all the world Is wait - ing some-where for

me, _____ Is wait - ing some - where, some - where for

me.

The sweet - est sounds I'll

ev - er hear Are still in - side my head.

The kind - est words I'll ev - er know Are

wait - ing to be said. The

most en - tranc - ing sight of all Is yet for

160

I CAN COOK TOO

from *On the Town*

Words and Music by LEONARD BERNSTEIN
Additional Choruses by BETTY COMDEN and ADOLPH GREEN

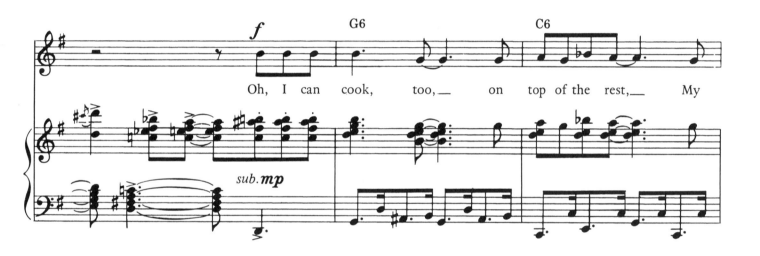

Oh, I can cook, too,__ on top of the rest,__ My

sea-food's the best__ in the town. Yes, I can cook, too,__ My

fish can't be beat,__ My sug-ar's the sweet - est a - round. I'm a

man's i - deal of a per - fect meal,__ Right down to the dem-i - tasse.__

I'm a pot of joy for a hun - gry boy,__

[Interlude]

Ba - by,   I'm   cook-in' with gas.___ Oh,   I'm   a

AS LONG AS HE NEEDS ME
from the Columbia Pictures-Romulus film *Oliver!*

Words and Music by
LIONEL BART

gone   But when he's near me _____ I don't let on _____ The way I

Tempo I

feel   in - side _____ The love I have   to   hide _____ The hell! I've

got   my   pride _____ As long as   he   needs   me.   He does-n't say the

things   he should   He acts the way   he   thinks   he should   But all the same   I'll

SHY
from *Once Upon a Mattress*

Words by MARSHALL BARER
Music by MARY RODGERS

And you may be sure: _____ way down deep I'm de-

mure. _____ Though some peo - ple I know might de - ny it, At

bot - tom I'm qui - et and pure! _____ I'm a - ware that it's

wrong _____ to be meek as I am; My chanc-es may pass me by. I pre-tend to be

Moderate 2

shy. _____ Though a

la - dy may be drip - ping with gla - mour, As

oft - en as not she - 'll stum - ble and stam - mer When

sud - den - ly con - front - ed with ro - mance. _____ And she's

oft - en she'll set - tle for some - thing less than the man of her

dreams. _____

I'm go - ing fish - ing for a mate.

I'm gon - na look in ev - 'ry nook.

But how much long-er must I wait   With

bait-ed breath and ho - ok?   And that is

why, _____ Though I'm pain-ful - ly shy, _____ I'm in-sane to know

Più mosso - Charleston beat

Which sir? ___ You, sir ___ Not you, sir. ___ Then who, sir? ___

IT'S A HELLUVA WAY TO RUN A LOVE AFFAIR

from *Plain and Fancy*

Words by ARNOLD B. HORWITT
Music by ALBERT HAGUE

Bounce tempo

-o!

He may a - dore me how would I know?

If I'm the light of his life ___ It does-n't show. ___ I go through the

mo-tions but I'm well a - ware It's a hell-u-va way to run a love af-

-fair. ___ He does-n't tin-gle when-ev-er we meet ___

Our love has all of the thrill ____ Of shredded wheat ____ We

nev - er run bare-foot through each oth - er's hair It's a hell-u-va way to

run a love af - fair! ____

1. Some luck-y lov-ers have a
2. One en-chant-ed eve-ning in my

ta - lent for ro - mance,   Hack-en-sack can seem like Par-is   France. ____
qui - et liv-ing room,   Can-dle lit and hea-vy with per - fume. ____

186

NEVER NEVER LAND
from *Peter Pan*

Lyrics by BETTY COMDEN
and ADOLPH GREEN
Music by JULE STYNE

PETER:

I know a place where

dreams are born, and time is nev - er planned. It's not on an - y chart, you must

find it with your heart. Nev - er Nev - er Land. It might be miles be -

yond the moon or right there where you stand. Just keep an o - pen mind, and then

sud-den-ly you'll find Nev - er Nev - er Land. You'll have a trea-sure if you

stay there, more pre-cious far than gold. For once you have found your

once you have found your way there, __ You can nev - er nev - er grow old.

So come with me where dreams are born, and time is nev - er planned.

Just think of love-ly things, and your heart will fly on wings for - ev - er __ in

Nev - er, Nev - er Land. _____

HOLD ON
from *The Secret Garden*

Lyrics by MARSHA NORMAN
Music by LUCY SIMON

Urgently

MARTHA:

What you've got to do is fin - ish what you have be - gun.

I don't know just how, but it's not o - ver 'til you've won. When you

(rit. a tempo)

do then, is you force your-self to wake up, and you say: It's this

dream, not me, that's bound to go a-way. Hold on, hold on, the

night will soon be by._____ Hold on, and think of some-thing else to try. Child, hold

on, there's an-gels on their way. Hold on and hear them say: Child, oh child, and it

years, what you do then is you tell your-self to wait it out. You

say: It's this day, not me, that's bound to go a-

way. Child, hold on, it's this day, not you, that's

broadening

bound to go a - way._____

molto rall.   *a tempo*   *rall.*   *sfz*

A TRIP TO THE LIBRARY
from *She Loves Me*

Lyrics by SHELDON HARNICK
Music by JERRY BOCK

MISS RITTER: *(Spoken before the introduction) Let me tell you, you've never seen anything like that library. So many books... so much marble... so quiet!*

sud-den-ly all of my con-fi-dence drib-bled a-way with a pit-i-ful plop. My

head was be-gin-ning to swim and my fore-head was cov-ered with cold per-spir-a-tion. I

started to reach for a book and my hand aut-o-mat-i-c'lly came to a stop.

I don't know how long I stood fro-zen, a vic-tim of pan-ic and mor-ti-fi - ca - tion.

With Freedom

Oh, _____ how I want-ed to flee _____ when a kind - ly voice, a

rall. **Moderato**

gen - tle voice whis-pered "Par-don me."

And there _ was this dear, sweet, clear-ly re-spec - ta-ble thick-ly be-spec - ta-cled

man who stood _ by my side and qui-et-ly said _ to me "Ma'am,

Don't mean _ to in - trude, but I was just won - der-ing are you in need _ of some

help?" I said "no... Yes, I am!"

The next___ thing I know I'm sip-ping hot choc-'late and

tell-ing my trou-bles to Paul, whose ten-der brown eyes kept send-ing com-pass-ion-ate

looks. A trip___ to the li-bra-ry_____ has made_ a new

girl of__ me,_____ for sud-den-ly I can__ see_____ the ma-gic of

books.

I

have to ad-mit in the back of my mind, I was pray-ing he would-n't get fresh.

And

all of the while I was won-der-ing why an il - lit - er-ate girl should at - tract him.

Then

all of a sud-den he said that I could-n't go wrong with "The Way of All Flesh."

Of

reading a - loud as I cook. As long as he's there to read there's quite a good

chance in - deed, a chance that I'll nev - er need to op - en a

Rubato

book! Un-like some-one else some-one I dim-ly re - call.

a tempo

I know he'll on-ly have eyes for me, my op - tom - e-trist Paul.

TELL ME ON A SUNDAY
from *Song and Dance*

Lyrics by DON BLACK
Music by ANDREW LLOYD WEBBER

cir - cus ring with a fly - ing trap - eze.___ Tell me on a Sun - day please.

I don't want to fight day and night, bad e - nough you're go - ing.

Don't leave in si - lence with no words at all.

Don't get drunk and slam the door, that's no way to end this. I

cresc.

know how I want you to say good-bye. Don't run off in the pour-ing rain. Don't call

f *ff*

me as they call your plane. Take the hurt out of all the pain. Take me to a park that's

rall. *mp* *slowly*

cov-ered with trees. __ Tell me on a Sun-day please. ___

p rall.

EVERYBODY LOVES LOUIS

from *Sunday in the Park with George*

Music and Lyrics by
STEPHEN SONDHEIM

Hel - lo, George . . . Where did you go, George? I know you're

near, George. I caught your eyes, George. I want your

ear, George. I've a sur - prise,

Lou - is al - ways is "there". Lou - is' thoughts are not

hard to fol - low, Lou - is' art is not hard to swal - low.

Not that Lou - is' per - fec - tion — That's what makes him i -

deal. Hard - ly an - y - thing worth ob - jec - tion:

*Actually, in the New York production, Dot stuffed her mouth with bread here, saying the last line with her mouth full.

IF HE REALLY KNEW ME

from *They're Playing Our Song*

Words by CAROLE BAYER SAGER
Music by MARVIN HAMLISCH